W9-BNK-650

Sol Levinson
& BROS., INC.

FUNERAL DIRECTORS

8900 REISTERSTOWN ROAD
PIKESVILLE, MARYLAND 21208
(410) 653-8900

GENTLE WILLOW
A Story for Children About Dying

by Joyce C. Mills, Ph.D.

illustrated by Michael Chesworth

Gareth Stevens Publishing
MILWAUKEE

For a free catalog describing Gareth Stevens' list of high-quality books, call 1-800-341-3569 (USA) or 1-800-461-9120 (Canada).

ISBN 0-8368-1070-8

Library edition published in 1994 by

Gareth Stevens Publishing
1555 North RiverCenter Drive, Suite 201
Milwaukee, Wisconsin 53212, USA

Copublished with Magination Press, an imprint of Brunner/Mazel, Inc., New York.
Text © 1994 by Joyce C. Mills, Ph.D. Illustrations © 1994 by Michael Chesworth.

All rights reserved. No part of this book may be reproduced or used in any form or by any means without permission in writing from Gareth Stevens, Inc.

Printed in the United States of America

1 2 3 4 5 6 7 8 9 99 98 97 96 95 94

Introduction for Parents, Teachers, and Librarians

Death and dying are difficult subjects for us, as adults, to deal with, let alone explain to children. While it is one thing to explain the death of an older person, such as a grandparent who has lived a full life, it is quite another to try to explain to a child the death of someone young, perhaps the same age as the child. It can be harder still to talk about death with a child who is himself/herself living with a life-threatening illness.

As adults, we search for the meaning of illnesses, such as cancer or AIDS, that shorten the precious life of a child. Children who personally face or who know people who are living with life-threatening illnesses have many questions: "Why is it happening to me?" or "Why does my friend have to die?" We may already have ideas or beliefs about the best way to talk with children about these important questions, but we may want additional help.

Born out of the inspirational *Little Tree*, a healing story for children who face serious medical problems, *Gentle Willow* was written for children who may not survive their illness and for the children who know them. This loving and tender story brings back the characters of Little Tree; Amanda the squirrel; and the two tree wizards, Fixumup and Imageen. These characters address feelings of disbelief, anger, and sadness along with love, compassion, and caregiving. *Gentle Willow* provides children, and those who are reading the story with them, a "transformational" way of viewing death and dying.

We all recognize that the greatest loss a parent can experience is the loss of a child. As parents or caregivers, we feel helpless when we are unable to effect a "cure" for our children. The story of *Gentle Willow* reminds us that although we may not have the medical cures, as yet, for many illnesses that affect the bodies of our children, we can still provide a loving atmosphere in which healing can occur on an emotional and spiritual level . . . and that stories and love are the healing medicines of the human soul.

It was the time of Spring once again, when all the flowers bloomed their brightest colors. It had been a long time since the big storm came through the forest where Little Tree and her friend Amanda lived and played.

Since that time, many new friends had come to live in the forest. Little Tree and Amanda especially liked Gentle Willow, who lived across the pond. Each day as the sun rose in the East, Little Tree rustled her leaves and sang "Good Morning" to her friends.

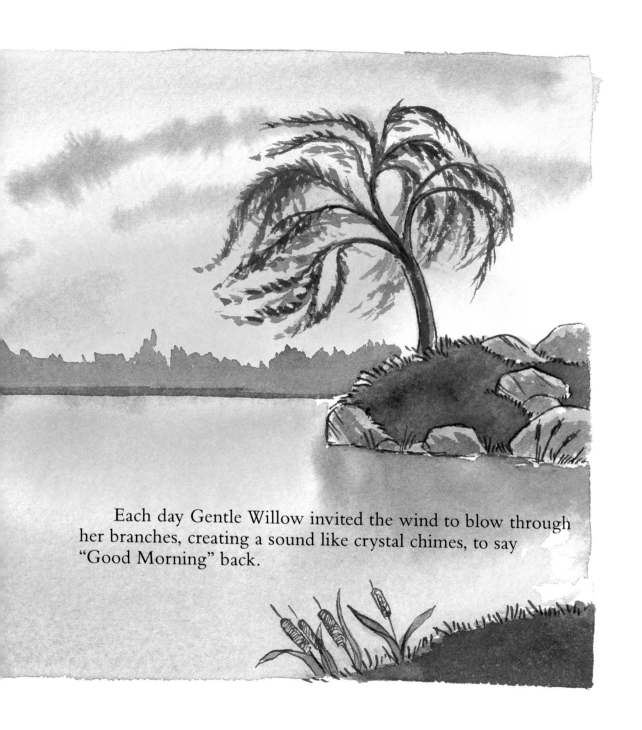

Each day Gentle Willow invited the wind to blow through her branches, creating a sound like crystal chimes, to say "Good Morning" back.

Amanda liked playing with Gentle Willow. Her new friend gave her places to store her nuts.

Amanda also liked to chase the big yellow butterflies who
danced within Gentle Willow's long and graceful branches.

One day, while Amanda was climbing up the trunk of Gentle Willow, she noticed that her friend looked different. Her bark was lumpy and bumpy. Her leaves were turning brown, and her branches were droopy.

"What is wrong, Gentle Willow?" asked Amanda.

"I don't know," whispered Gentle Willow. "I just feel different."

"Don't worry," said Amanda. "Tomorrow you will feel better."

But many tomorrows came, and Gentle Willow still did not feel better.

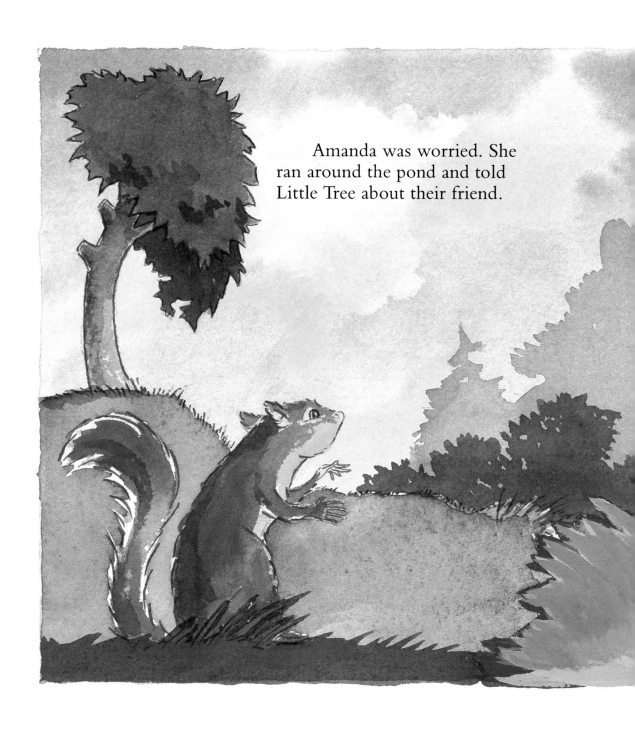

Amanda was worried. She ran around the pond and told Little Tree about their friend.

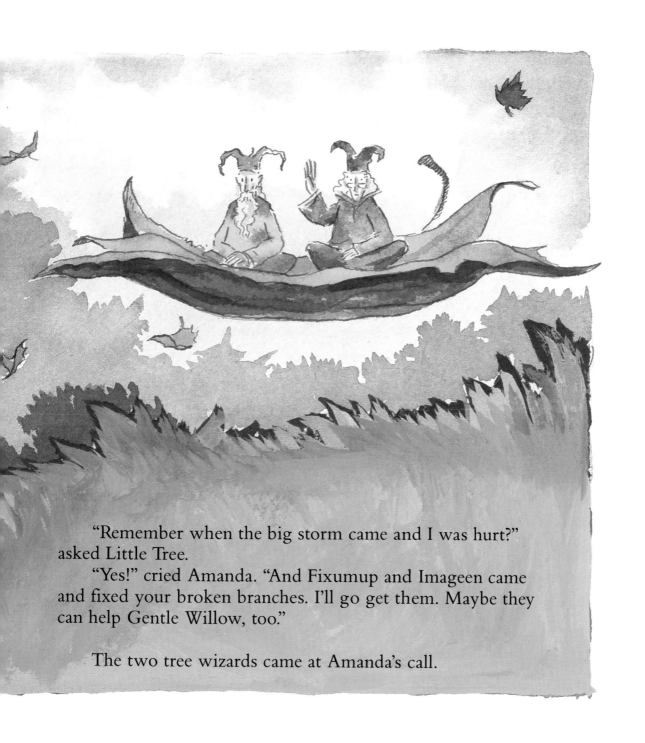

"Remember when the big storm came and I was hurt?"
asked Little Tree.

"Yes!" cried Amanda. "And Fixumup and Imageen came
and fixed your broken branches. I'll go get them. Maybe they
can help Gentle Willow, too."

The two tree wizards came at Amanda's call.

Fixumup checked Gentle Willow's branches and her lumpy, bumpy bark. Imageen looked closely at her roots. Amanda stayed close. The butterflies danced all around Gentle Willow, while Little Tree watched from across the pond.

After all the checking, Imageen and Fixumup went to the knowing rock by the pond to talk. Amanda followed.

"What is wrong with Gentle Willow?" she asked.

"Your friend's hurt is different from the hurt Little Tree had because of the storm," said Fixumup. "Gentle Willow has something we have seen before in the forest, but we cannot make it go away."

"What do you mean?" Amanda yelled. "You HAVE to help Gentle Willow. You HAVE to make her better. YOU ARE THE TREE WIZARDS OF THE FOREST!"

"Yes," said Imageen sadly, "we are Tree Wizards. But there are some things even Tree Wizards cannot fix. We can give Gentle Willow tree sap to help her feel stronger. We can give her herbs to help her feel comfortable. But we cannot make her all better."

"What will happen to her?" asked Amanda.

"Gentle Willow will look different as time goes by," said Imageen. "She will need all of our help every day. We can sing her songs and tell her stories. Each of our songs and each of our stories will help her feel a special medicine called Love."

Amanda, Fixumup and Imageen went together to tell Little Tree about Gentle Willow.

"We are losing our friend," cried Little Tree. "What will we do without her?"

"You are right, Little Tree," said Imageen. "You won't know or see Gentle Willow as you know her now. She is going on a journey of changing forms. Human people call it dying. But all the years you have known Gentle Willow, she has been giving you special gifts."

"Gifts?" asked Amanda and Little Tree.

"Yes. Special gifts called memories. Memories of her crystal chimes. . .memories of waving good morning. . .memories of laughing with the wind. . .memories of special times you've shared together. The time will come when all of us who live in the forest will sing a special song to say 'Goodbye' to Gentle Willow as we know her today. And the time will come when we will recognize her in another way. Maybe it will be in a song from the wind. Maybe it will be in the dance of the butterflies. I don't know. But each of you will know in your own special way."

Every day Little Tree looked across the pond and rustled her leaves to sing songs to Gentle Willow. And every day Amanda visited and told her stories. One day, while Amanda was visiting, Gentle Willow began to cry.

"I am afraid to change. I want to stay the way I am. I want to stay a tree."

Not knowing how to help her friend, Amanda sat quietly.
She just listened, and stayed close, while Gentle Willow wept.
Then Amanda remembered about songs and stories. . .and
love. As she was trying to think of a good story, one of the big
yellow butterflies fluttered by. Amanda snuggled closer to
Gentle Willow and began her story.

"Once a long time ago, when Yellow Butterfly was little, she was something called a caterpillar. She was fuzzy and long and crawled on the ground, over rocks and flowers.

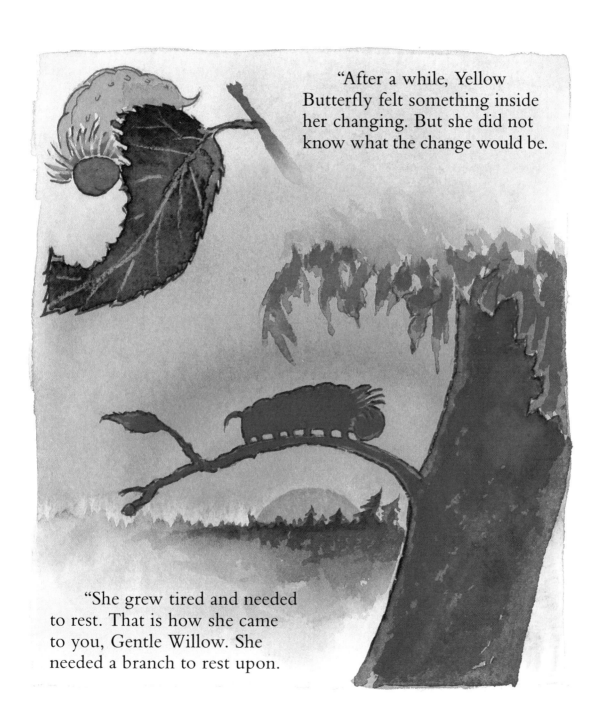

"After a while, Yellow Butterfly felt something inside her changing. But she did not know what the change would be.

"She grew tired and needed to rest. That is how she came to you, Gentle Willow. She needed a branch to rest upon.

"Butterfly began to spin a warm blanket around herself. Inside of the blanket it was verrrry dark. Yellow Butterfly felt her whole fuzzy caterpillar self changing shape.

"After what seemed a very long time, she felt ready to come out of the blanket. She did not want to be in that darkness anymore.

"So, using all her strength,
Yellow Butterfly pushed herself
out into the light.

"And there she was.

"Not crawling on the ground anymore. . . not a fuzzy caterpillar anymore. Instead, she had silken yellow wings. Her whole form had changed. And, as she flew, she found all the other butterflies just like herself."

When Amanda finished the story, she noticed that Gentle
Willow had stopped crying. She seemed to be smiling a quiet
understanding.

It was the time of Spring once again, when all the flowers bloomed their brightest colors. Little Tree and Amanda looked across the pond to the place where Gentle Willow once stood.

"Look," said Little Tree. "The big yellow butterflies have come back to dance."

"Yes," said Amanda. "Perhaps, in a different way, they still hear the crystal songs of our friend Gentle Willow."

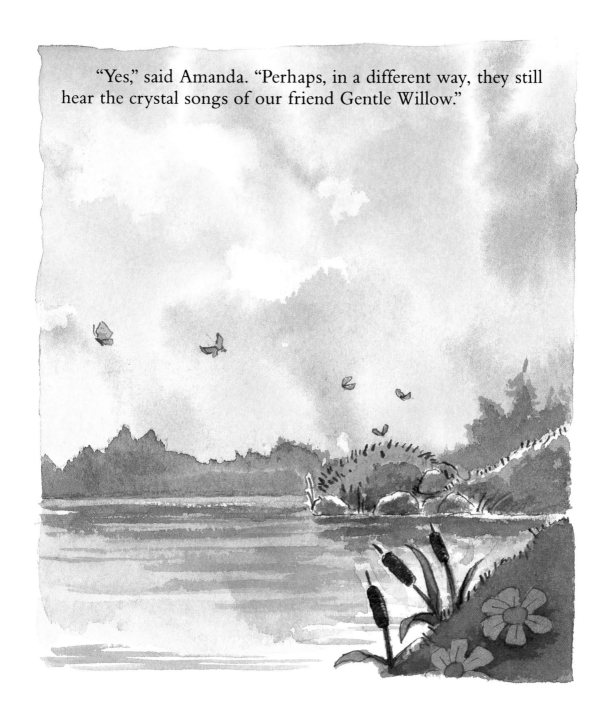

FOR MORE INFORMATION . . .

Books

Cartoon Magic: How to Help Children Discover Their Rainbows Within.
Crowley and Mills (Magination)

Little Tree: A Story for Children with Serious Medical Problems.
Mills (Magination)[2]

Sammy's Mommy Has Cancer.
Kohlenberg (Gareth Stevens)

Therapeutic Metaphors for Children and the Child Within.
Mills and Crowley (Brunner/Mazel)[1]

The Three Birds.
Van den Berg (Gareth Stevens)

Videotape

PEI: Tangled in a Threat. Animated short for young children that deals with feelings of fear, separation, and curiosity about death.

Exercises

Children who are living with life-threatening illnesses often experience both pain and fear. Positive imagery can be a powerful tool to help children feel more in control of their physical and emotional discomfort. The **My Pain Getting Better Book**[1] exercise is a simple and fun technique. Have the child draw a picture of the pain or fear. Next have her/him draw how that picture looks feeling "all better." Then, have her/him draw what might change the first picture into the second picture. These three simple steps help children separate from pain or fear and call upon their inner "healing helpers" to create a symbol of "all better" or relief. **The Magic Happy Breath**[2] exercise can also help a child feel more comfortable. Ask the child to close his/her eyes and take a deep, slow breath in through the nose and out through the mouth, as if gently blowing a feather. Next, ask the child to imagine the third picture (from the previous exercise) "going inside," right to the place of the hurt or afraid feeling until it is changed into the second, "all better" picture.

Index